Caillou®

The Birthday Party

Adaptation of the animated series: Claire St-Onge
Illustrations: Eric Sévigny, based on the animated series

Today is Caillou's birthday.
Mommy and Daddy have
decorated the house with balloons
and streamers. It looks wonderful!
Caillou can't wait. His friends are
coming to celebrate with him.
"When will Leo and Clementine
be here?"
"Soon, Caillou," Mommy says.
"Let's get the cake ready while
we wait."

Mommy has made Caillou's favorite cake.
"Caillou, would you like to help me clean the bowl?" Mommy asks.
"Yes, please, Mommy!" says Caillou. He scrapes the icing from the bowl with the big spatula. He smiles as he licks the sweet icing.

Rosie comes into the kitchen and sees the yummy icing. "I want some!" she says.
"Let Rosie have a taste, Caillou," says Daddy. He dips his finger into the bowl.
"I thought you said that Caillou should let Rosie have some," says Mommy.
Caillou giggles when he hears Mommy scolding Daddy!

It's time for Caillou to open his present from Grandma. Caillou has told everyone that he wants a new dinosaur for his birthday. Did Grandma remember? Caillou opens the big box, hoping there is a dinosaur inside. Caillou is disappointed when he sees that Grandma's gift is a sweater.

Caillou hears the doorbell ring
and runs to the door.
"Clementine! Leo!" shouts Caillou.
Everyone is here now.
Clementine and Leo have both
brought a gift. Caillou is impatient
to find out what's inside the boxes.
"The gifts are for later, Caillou. It's
time to go into the living room for
games," Mommy announces.

Daddy takes out the face-painting
kit. He starts to draw a circle
around Caillou's eye.
"Stay still just a little longer, Caillou.
I'm almost done," Daddy says.
"It feels funny, Daddy!" says
Caillou. He giggles at the tickly
feeling of the brush on his cheeks.
He can't see the whiskers Daddy is
painting.

Caillou, Rosie, Clementine, and Leo are having fun in the kitchen. There are treats to eat, and they all have painted faces. Caillou looks just like his cat, Gilbert!

Here comes Caillou's birthday cake!
"Happy birthday, Caillou!"
everyone shouts. Caillou can't wait
to blow out the candles.
"First you have to make a wish,"
Grandma says.
Caillou knows exactly what to wish
for: a new dinosaur! He takes
a deep breath and blows out the
candles with all his might.

Caillou has eaten all the cake he
can. Mommy and Daddy give him
a big box.
"Happy birthday, Caillou!" they
say. Caillou unwraps the box as
fast as he can.
"Wow, my dinosaur!" says
Caillou, hugging his new toy.
"Thank you!"

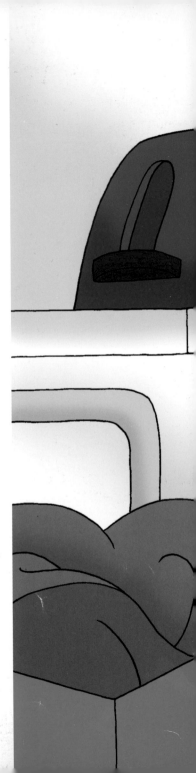

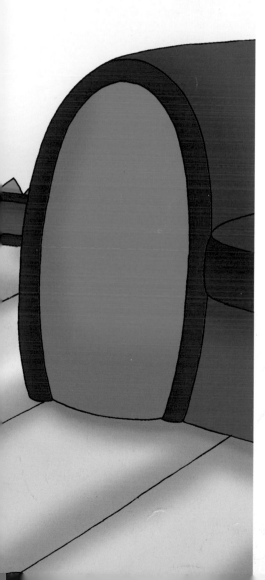

"Rosie, look what you did!" says
Caillou, pointing to a big blob of
ice cream on his shirt.
"It's okay, Caillou," Mommy says.
"Rosie didn't do it on purpose."
"Here's a clean sweater for you
to wear," Grandma says. She
takes Caillou's new sweater out of
the box and holds it up.

"Wow!" Caillou is surprised to see that his new birthday sweater has a dinosaur on it! He quickly takes off his shirt and pulls on the sweater.

"It's another birthday dinosaur!" says Caillou, smiling. "This is my best birthday ever!"

Text: adaptation by Claire St-Onge of the animated series CAILLOU,
produced by DHX Media Inc.
All rights reserved.
Original story written by Matthew Cope
Original Episode # 19: Caillou's Birthday Present
Illustrations: Eric Sévigny, based on the animated series CAILLOU

The PBS KIDS logo is a registered mark of PBS and is used with permission.

We acknowledge the financial support of the Government of Canada through
the Canada Book Fund for our publishing activities.

Canadian   Patrimoine
Heritage   canadien

We acknowledge the support of the Ministry of Culture and Communications
of Quebec and SODEC for the publication and promotion of this book.

SODEC
Québec

Bibliothèque et Archives nationales du Québec and Library and Archives
Canada cataloguing in publication

St-Onge, Claire, 1960-
[Caillou: l'anniversaire. English]
Caillou: the birthday party
Second edition.
(Clubhouse)
Translation of: Caillou fête son anniversaire.
For children aged 3 and up.

ISBN 978-2-89718-122-2

1. Birthdays - Juvenile literature. 2. Gifts - Juvenile literature. I. Sévigny, Éric.
II. Title. III. Title: Caillou: l'anniversaire. English. IV. Series: Clubhouse.

GT2430.S2413 2014   j394.2   C2013-941967-5

Printed in China
10 9 8 7 6 5 4 3 2 1   CHO1898 NOV2014